# Dewey Doo-it™
## Helps Owlie Fly Again

A Musical Storybook
Inspired by

**Christopher Reeve**

With Songs & Narration by

**Mandy Patinkin**

**Bernadette Peters**

**Dana Reeve**

By Brahm Wenger & Alan Green

Illustrated by Jean Gillmore

Songs by Brahm Wenger & John M. Rosenberg

*For Christopher Reeve —*
*whose courageous steps in battling paralysis*
*have inspired us all.*

Photo: Dana Fineman

*"May flights of angels sing thee to thy rest."*
— Shakespeare

Library of Congress Control Number: Dewey Doo-it Helps Owlie Fly Again 0-9745143-1-4  2004095743

Dewey Doo-it is a registered trademark of The Helpful Doo-its Project LLC.
Published by RandallFraser Publishing
2082 Business Center Drive, Suite 163
Irvine, CA 92612  866-339-3999
Printed in the United States of America

"OH NO!" Dewey Doo-it yelled, as he watched his brand new kite plunge to the ground—for the third time that morning.

Dewey was not having a good day. "All my friends can fly their kites," he said.
But no matter how hard he tried, *Dewey Doo-it just couldn't do it.*

"You're doing it all wrong," said Howie Doo-it, Dewey's older brother. "You have to fly the kite with the '*Thing-a-ma-jiggies*' hanging off the end, like this."

Dewey's little sister Anita Doo-it came over to help, too. Now, Dewey knew what to do.

He ran, pulling his kite...

until suddenly...

his kite started pulling *him!*

Right into a big…

…TREE! C R U N C H! This was a very tall tree.

"I can't climb that high!" Dewey said.

"We should go ask Owlie for help," suggested Kenya Doo-it.

"Good idea! Let's go find him," said the twins, Woody Doo-it and Willie Doo-it.

"He can fly up there and get it down, for sure."

Their friend Owlie could be flying anywhere. He loved to flap his long, graceful wings and fly all over the Jingle Jangle Jungle.

But when the Doo-its found Owlie, he wasn't flying, he wasn't flapping his wings. He was sitting in a *wheelchair*, dreaming of flying. Everyone fell silent. For a moment, the Doo-its just stood there, not knowing what to say.

Dewey touched the wheelchair. "What happened, Owlie?" he asked.

Anita was oddly shy too. "Why are you holding the brush in your beak?"

"I had an accident," Owlie replied. He slowly let the brush fall to his lap. "I can no longer flap my wings and fly the way I used to. So for now, I use this wheelchair, and when I paint, I hold my brush this way."

"But I can still do lots of things," Owlie said. "I can use my special computer whenever I like. I just *tell* it what to do."

"I can whistle, I can sing, and I can even zoom through the Jingle Jangle Jungle and visit all my friends."

But the truth was, sometimes Owlie still felt sad. "I do miss flapping my wings," he sighed. He looked up at Dewey's kite stuck in the big tree. "I'd really love to fly up and get your kite down for you."

"Then fly again you will, my friend!" said Dewey.
He tied some '*Thing-a-ma-jiggies*' to Owlie's wings and legs and took
off across the park. Dewey tried again and again to fly Owlie like a kite…

…with very little success.
(He did, however, succeed in carving out a very large hole in the ground.)

"That's not going to work," Howie explained. "Owlie's not a kite, he's an owl."
"I know," said Dewey, "but we have to find a way to help Owlie fly again."
Everyone agreed. Everyone wanted to help.

There was lots of work to be done.

"First, Owlie has to learn how to flap his wings again," said Howie. "We need to build him a *Ga-Liftin and Ga-Flappin* machine!"

"A *Ga-Liftin and Ga-Flappin* machine?" asked Kenya. "How do we build that?"

"I know!" said Willie. He reached into his pocket. "Look, I have the plans right here!"

The Doo-its studied the big blue drawings, trying to make sense of all the funny squiggles and curvy lines. Finally, Dewey declared, "Ropes and springs, gears—big and small. We have these things, we have them all! What are we waiting for? Let's go build it!"

Owlie thought he was ready, but Dewey knew there was more to do.
"Almost," he said. "Almost."

Next, the Doo-its made a nice soft 'pillow' in the sandbox so Owlie could learn how to land safely on the ground.

"Here I come!" yelled Owlie, as he sailed through the air. "I'm landing! I'm landing!"

With each practice landing, Owlie's confidence grew.
"Now I *know* I'm ready to fly up and get Dewey's kite down."

Dewey agreed. "And look," he said, "Willie brought along something special to help you fly."
Everyone hurried over to the see-saw for the big lift off.

"Uh-oh!" Owlie was having second thoughts.
But it was a little too late for that…

B O O M!
Owlie shot off the see-saw like a little cannonball and flew straight into the sky.
"I'm flying!" Owlie yelled. "*It's different*, but I'm flying!"

He flew up, up, up, to the big tree and knocked Dewey's kite loose from the high branch.

Everyone cheered, "Hurray for Owlie! HURRAY!"

At last, Dewey could fly his kite in the park with all his friends. He was so happy. But when he saw Owlie flying by, he realized there was something much more important than flying his kite. Dewey and Owlie had actually helped each other. Dewey got his kite back, and Owlie, in his own special way, saw his dream come true.

"Thank you, Owlie," said a grateful Dewey.
"No, thank *you*," Owlie replied, as he soared high in the sky. "Thank you everyone for *helping Owlie fly again!*"

# Hi Everyone!

This story was inspired by someone else who used a wheelchair. His name is Christopher Reeve and he was one of the country's leading movie actors. Christopher loved to ride horses but one day when he was riding, he had an accident that left him paralyzed from his neck down. After that, he used a wheelchair. But just like Owlie, Christopher had a lot of helpful Doo-its around him who tried to help him move his arms and legs again.

Christopher knew that he wasn't the only one who wanted to walk again, so he started an organization called the *Christopher Reeve Paralysis Foundation* to find the cure for paralysis and help the millions of people who use wheelchairs. Now, scientists are closer than ever to finding cures and treatments for paralysis. The *Christopher Reeve Paralysis Foundation* also works to improve the day-to-day lives of people with disabilities.

Photo: Ken Regan

Sadly, Christopher passed away in 2004, but his example of courage and determination in the face of great personal tragedy continues to inspire all those who are working to cure paralysis.

Thanks, **Dewey**

To make a donation, visit:
www.crpf.org
or call 1-800-225-0292